Friendsgiving with Benefits

Holiday Pact Book One

Lizzie B Brown

Proofread by Emily Michel.

Cover by The Red Fox Creative.

Contents

To all the people behind the scenes who supported me in one way or another, thank you. I wouldn't have accomplished this without any of you.

Message to Readers

This story is about side characters that appear in my romance serials The Bucket List and Obedience. You do not need to read either romance serial before jumping into this story because it is a prequel that takes place one year prior to the beginning of The Bucket List and Obedience.

Content Warning

Mental health is important. While not everyone needs content warnings, there are those who do. You can find the most up to date content warnings on my website: https://www.lizzieb-brown.com/content-warnings

Prologue

The Joke

Nixon

Early October

If Poppy Madison Harper wanted to do something, nothing could get in her way. Soft lips wrapped around my cock as the most perfect mouth sucked me off. With eyes closed, my head fell back, gently bumping the wall behind me as a contented sigh escaped my lips. I had the best friend in the entire universe. I didn't care what anyone said.

Earlier in the day, I ran into Cherry, my latest ex. The end of a year-long relationship had been hard enough, but seeing her being so cozy with Theo out in public was worse, considering he was the reason we broke up...sort of.

Of course, I was a wreck at first, but after a month I was feeling like myself again. That was until I saw *her* with *him*. It was like salt in a fresh wound, all the insecurities from that night rising to the surface.

I texted Poppy for support, not expecting more than a cuddle when I got home. So naturally I was surprised when she jumped me as soon as I walked through the door. She didn't even take my pants off, pulling my cock out and getting to work as soon as my fly was down.

Not that I was complaining. I would take a BJ from my favorite person over anything Cherry and I ever did. Theo could fucking have her.

It was his name Cherry called out when *my* head was buried between her thighs on our one-year anniversary. Of course, I assumed she was cheating, but the truth was strangely worse.

When the dust settled and the shouting stopped, she confessed that every time we fooled around she was thinking of someone else. Sometimes it was a celebrity, sometimes a guy she knew, but never ever me. Who did that?

I ended things that night, despite all Cherry's pleading. We were good together, real good, but I couldn't be with someone who was a million miles away with their fantasy during our most intimate moments. I deserved someone who was present.

Poppy's nails dug into the thighs of my jeans as she worked to take me deeper and deeper until I hit the back of her throat. You would think my piercings would get in the way, and they probably did, but that didn't stop her.

She moaned around my shaft, the feel of the vibrations on my cock sending me into overdrive. I could barely stand, overcome with pleasure. If she kept this up, I was going to come way too fast.

Don't forget to watch, I reminded myself. Poppy loved being watched. She was a performer at heart who loved the spotlight. If I wanted a wildcat in bed, all I had to do was tape us having sex. Give my girl an audience, and she became the perfect little porn star.

Forcing my eyes open, looked down at my best friend, who was going to town on my cock like it was her favorite meal. Her face was a mess, her mascara running from all the tears, as she pushed herself to the limit. I wish half the people I dated had a fraction of her talent sucking sausage. Everyone thinks I'm such a giver. Nope, I just hate bad head.

Our eyes locked, and as predicted, Poppy kicked into full porn star, moaning and gagging as she choked me down. There was hot, and then there was Poppy trying to take my entire length hot.

Not to brag, but I was big, too big for Poppy to fit every inch of me in her mouth kind of big. We tried plenty of times. It wasn't possible. I knew that, but watching her so desperate to take all of me anyway was my weakness.

My balls tightened as the familiar feeling of my climax came barreling through me far too soon.

"Fuck. Fuck. Fuck," I murmured as I took a fistful of her long, brown hair and yanked her head back.

With one hand holding Poppy firmly in position, I used the other to grab my cock and aim as my orgasm burst through me. My girl opened wide and stuck out her tongue as my cum splattered all over her face. After over a decade of friendship with benefits, she knew exactly what I liked.

I stroked myself through the aftershocks, making sure every drop decorated her pretty face. Poppy held still in my grasp as I panted for breath. Without even thinking, I did what I always did when I painted a piece of her with my cum. I grabbed my phone from my pocket and snapped a pic. *Another one for the special Poppy spank bank folder.*

Still riding the high, I looked down at my friend. She looked perfect, kneeling before me covered in my spunk. If this could be my every day, I would truly be in heaven.

"Marry me," I said, despite knowing her response would pop my blissful bubble of contentment.

Poppy laughed as she pulled her shirt up to clean her face. She always laughed. I released my hold and helped her to her feet, holding in the disappointment that had become a part of our routine.

"You say that every time I blow you. If you're not careful, I might just say yes," she teased.

Oh, no. Marrying my best friend? How horrible!

"Please don't. Then we'd really be stuck together," I replied with a teasing smile to hide the pain I felt in my heart. *Coward.*

I held my smile until she left the room to change her shirt. The rejection never dulled. Not that I blamed Poppy. Who would take a guy seriously when he only confessed his feelings after a blow job? Maybe if she knew I only said it to her.

I used to hold out hope that we would become more. We lived together. We fucked occasionally. Our friends joked we were the perfect couple, but we weren't together.

Poppy didn't see me like that, or maybe she didn't ever want to settle down. I wasn't really sure since that was the only conversation we never had. I was too afraid of what the answer might be.

Poppy was my soulmate, the one person I couldn't live without. Even if we both got married to other people, we would still live together in some fashion. She was sold on the idea of a duplex or communal house if one of us actually settled down. I agreed enthusiastically every time because I couldn't stand the thought of living without her friendship. Even if the sex went away, I needed her friendship.

And so we continued to live together and occasionally fuck, and the only time my real feelings slipped was when she dropped to her knees for me. It was easier that way.

Chapter 1

Early Morning Preparations

Poppy

Thanksgiving Morning

My eyes burned as tears blurred my vision and ran down my cheeks. Onions were the bane of my existence, but I used them in a lot of my cooking. Thanksgiving was no exception. I needed to chop at least five, but my vision was long gone halfway through the first one.

Plow through it, Poppy. You've got a lot to get done today, and these onions won't chop themselves.

I was so wrapped up in my epic onion quest that I didn't notice the familiar presence creeping up behind me until I felt his warm hand on my shoulder.

"Move, Pops. I got this. Go prep something else," Nixon ordered, taking the knife from me.

When did he wake up? Not that I wasn't grateful, but I purposely slipped out of bed without waking him so he could get a few more hours. There was no reason for us both to be up at six in the morning.

"Thanks, Nixy," I said as I blindly made my way to the kitchen sink.

Turning on the warm water, I washed my hands and then my face, trying to free myself from the onion's evil clutches. *Stupid onions.* If Nixon hadn't walked in the kitchen when he did, I would have been a crying, snotty mess by onion two. I could have lost a finger by onion three if I kept chopping in that state. Thank God he didn't sleep in, I guess.

"How much prep is there this morning?" he asked, keeping his eyes on his task. The way he chopped the onions made me think of those props on the cooking shows we sometimes watched together.

Nixon in the kitchen was always a treat. Cooking was one of his hobbies and he was damn good at it, but this morning he was a different kind of treat. Standing in the kitchen in only gray sweatpants and thick-rimmed glasses with sleep rumpled hair, he was a sight to be seen.

Everyone was always surprised the first time they saw Nixon without a shirt, and I was no different. Because of his frame and the stereotypes of geeks in glasses, everyone assumed he'd be scrawny and all bones. Nope. My Nixy was all lean, toned muscles covered in vibrant ink. *And a magical cock. Can't forget that.*

I could stare at Nixon's tattoos for hours. My favorite was the twin NES Zappers on his pelvis, a nerdy play on the more traditional pistol pelvic tattoos some men had. With his sweatpants hanging low, I could see the normally hidden tattoos peeking out.

If he wasn't holding a knife, I might have been tempted to pull his pants down further to get a closer look at the whole thing.

"I did most of the tedious stuff last night. I just need to boil the noodles, shred a couple blocks of cheese, and then throw each dish in the oven," I explained once I stopped drooling.

We only had the one oven, and most of my holiday recipes were casseroles, which made Thanksgiving interesting. We'd worked out the kinks over the years, and by now I had a pretty good idea how to pace the baking so everything would be ready before guests arrived.

"Ugh, the cheese is the most tedious part! Why can't you just buy the pre-shredded stuff?" Nixon whined while he chopped.

I rolled my eyes. Why did he care? He wasn't the one who would shred three blocks of sharp cheddar.

"Cellulose powder," I answered.

"What?" He paused chopping long enough to shoot me a confused look.

"Cellulose powder. It's the white powder all over packaged shredded cheese to keep it from clumping together. I don't notice it on taco night, but I swear it mucks up the mac and cheese," I explained.

I stopped using pre-shredded cheese two years prior. The convenience wasn't worth whatever it was doing to the food, even if I was the only one who noticed. I didn't cook often, most of our meals were prepared by Nixon or takeout, but when I did cook, I wanted to enjoy it.

Nixon let out a frustrated huff, frowning at the onions as he chopped away. What was with him this morning?

Last night he was his typical happy self, the calm in my pre-Thanksgiving Day storm. A lot of people assumed I was the calm and collected one out of the two of us, but under the surface was chaos. When left alone, I was impulsive and quick to panic. Like last night, when I almost had a meltdown cutting the broccoli. Then Nixon stepped in, helped me finish the prep, and kept my mind occupied.

The best part was when we finished cleaning up. I knew I was forgetting something, but I couldn't figure out what. (Spoiler alert: it was the onions). No matter how hard I tried, I couldn't remember, and it drove me crazy. Nixon's solution? He dragged me to his bedroom and edged me for half an hour. By the time he let me come, I was exhausted and fell right to sleep.

After a night like that, he was usually sunshine and rainbows the next day. Maybe it was because I was the only one who got a happy ending? Except that wasn't like Nixon. He'd take matters into his own hands, literally, after I fell asleep.

"Everything alright, buddy?" I asked as I grabbed the blocks of cheese from the fridge.

"Buddy?" He raised an eyebrow and smirked.

"Yeah, pal. What's got you blue this morning?" I probed in an overly sweet voice as I moved around the kitchen, grabbing a cheese grater and bowl.

Normally, a little goofy conversation was enough to bring Nixon out of one of his moods, but this morning was different for some reason. He scoffed at the onion and shook his head in disbelief, which meant this wasn't one of his normal moody fits.

"Oh, I don't know, Pops. Maybe it has something to do with the fact that I fell asleep with my best friend in my arms, but then I woke up this morning to an empty bed," he said with a twinge of bitterness.

You know better than to slip out of bed the next morning. That I did, but I had to get a start on the day and waking him so early seemed rude.

I loved Nixon to death. He was my best friend, my rock, the one almost constant that I could usually depend on. He was also quite sensitive and wore his heart on his sleeve. Part of my job as his BFF was to guard that fragile little heart of his from those that might take advantage, either on purpose or accident. That's part of why we had a bad decision insurance agreement between us.

It was a friends-with-benefits arrangement that said if we were both single, we'd turn to each other before a one-night stand with a rando. The benefits were obvious, knowing who you were fucking being the big one. We'd known each other almost a decade and were very familiar with each other's bodies. It also meant that I didn't have to doll myself up and hustle at a club or bar just to get laid. My own personal boy toy was only a bedroom away.

The arrangement was great for Nixon because I knew what to expect. He often got attached when things got physical. Post sex cuddles were a requirement immediately after, and sometimes the next morning. If you didn't know him, he could easily appear needy or clingy, but that was just Nixon.

His current mood was a perfect example of why this thing worked between us. I'd seen what happened when someone reacted poorly to one of his needy moods. They'd freak out, pull back, and leave him hurt. Me? I knew you just had to ride it out, and he'd be over it within the hour.

"Sorry, Nixy. You know I had to get things moving this morning. There was no reason for us both to be up at six," I said, trying to reason with him.

He grumbled in response as he finished up the onions. Whatever. He would be fine once our guests arrived, and the house was full of people to keep him occupied.

Speaking of keeping Nixon occupied...

"Rupert will be here. He's super excited about his first American Thanksgiving. Maybe you can give him one to remember," I said, hoping to steer the conversation elsewhere.

Nixon let out an annoyed sigh. I didn't even have to look at him to know he was rolling his eyes, too. *Moody boy.*

"You're the one who's got it bad for British accents," he shot back.

True, but I wasn't the one who spent the last two weeks laughing at every corny joke told by our friend from across the pond. Nixon could lie to himself, but not to me. The energy between the two of them was electric, and I wasn't the only one who noticed. People were taking bets on which one of them would make the first move.

Completely unaware of my thoughts, Nixon came up behind me and grabbed my hips. I tried to ignore the raging hard-on while I grated the cheese, but it was difficult with him grinding it against my ass. *Someone's excited this morning.* He moved my hair to the side, gently kissing up my neck until his lips brushed the shell of my ear.

"And even if I *was* into him, it wouldn't matter until January, right?" he whispered.

A knowing smile crossed my lips. The Holiday Pact. It was an extension of our bad decision insurance. No new relationships from November until after the new year. It had been a few years since we were both single during the holiday season, so I had honestly forgotten about it. Suddenly, his behavior the last couple weeks made a lot more sense. He was working under the impression we were a faux couple.

Better not let him figure out that I forgot. That would be awful. Especially since he was still hurting over Cherry. That little bitch fucked him in the head. My poor Nixy had needed lots of extra assurance since that sour tart.

"Right?" There was a slight edge to his voice this time.

And there it was. That brief twinge of panic he tried to hide made my heart break. If that bitch and I ever crossed paths, I'd kick her ass for making him feel like he wasn't good enough.

Nixon's fingers dug into my hips, demanding my attention. I wiggled my ass against his erection, causing him to drop his head on my shoulder and moan. *Maybe he didn't take care of himself last night.*

"Right, Nixy. But that doesn't mean you can't butter him up for January, right?" I asked.

"I don't care about January. All I want is you on all fours while I make you scream my name," he said between gritted teeth.

"As nice as that sounds, I have things to do. You know how tight the schedule is today," I argued calmly. It was important for Nixon not to feel rejected, but the thought of running behind filled me to the brim with anxiety.

Nixon reached past me and grabbed the block of cheese from my hand before shoving me out of the way.

"Excuse me, what do you think you are doing?!" I snapped. If this was his idea of foreplay, I was so not into it.

"Helping you get ahead of schedule," he replied without looking in my direction.

I opened my mouth to argue, but thought better of it. While I wanted him to relax, I really needed the help. Running ahead of schedule was also very appealing, as was fitting in a little fun.

"Thanks," I muttered, moving to the next task.

Nixon gave a little grunt and nodded. Neither one of us was exactly happy, but it was enough for the moment. Once I had a better handle on meal prep, I could relax and give Nixon the extra attention he needed.

Chapter 2

Distractions

Poppy

Stepping out of the shower, I grabbed my towel and quickly dried off before wrapping it around my hair. Any other day, a shower would take me close to an hour. Something about the hot water pouring over me made it easy to shut my brain off and recenter myself. It was my moment of Zen.

Not today, though. My mind kept replaying everything I still had to get done before company arrived. I knew I would get it all done, I always did, but until every dish was ready, I would continue to stress.

My nerves were so amped up that I rushed through my shower so I could get back out to the food. *Everything is fine. Nixon is watching the oven for you*, I reminded myself. That was all fine and dandy, but I needed to be the one there. Nixon was a skilled cook, but he didn't know my family's recipes like I did.

Moving from my en suite bathroom into my bedroom, I froze, greeted by the image of Nixon laid out naked on my bed with his cock in hand. His eyes met mine through the lenses of his nerd boy glasses, holding me in his intense stare, daring me to watch as he leisurely stroked himself.

Great. No one is watching the food.

Frustration bubbled up inside me. This wasn't a random day off where we could just fuck around. It was Thanksgiving! We had over twenty guests expected in a few hours, and I still had so much to do between the food, the setup, and getting myself ready. Nixon knew how important today was.

"The mac and cheese—" I began to protest, but Nixon was quick to cut me off.

"Already dinged. I took it out and popped your cornbread dressing in. We've got time, Pops. Come play with me." He patted the empty space next to him on the bed.

My eyes roamed down Nixon's decorated body as I contemplated his request. He was lean, sculpted muscle wrapped in colorful ink, like a sexy piece of art. *My* sexy piece of art.

I've spent countless hours studying the various pieces on his body. The right sleeve was a collage of his favorite 8-bit video games, while the left was a few panels of his favorite Spider-Man comic. Both were so intricate that years later, I would still notice something new. His left pec had a pixelated heart that I often teased him for. It was so goofy, but very fitting for someone who did so little to shield his heart.

My gaze trailed further down his body, past the pelvic tattoo I loved so much, until I reached his rock hard erection. Nixon didn't have an abnormally large cock by any means, but he was eight inches and thicker than you'd imagine. Between his girth and the piercings, we always needed a lot of foreplay for it to fit inside me.

When we first met, Nixon only had the apadravya, a vertical bar pierced through the head. I admit it fascinated the hell out of me when he whipped it out at a party the weekend we met. One of his friends teased him about it, then one of my friends begged him to show us, and he pulled it out like his cock was some party trick. Back then, he was a lot less shy about whipping it out in a crowd.

Since then, he added the frenum and another vertical bar a little further down his shaft that I never remembered the name of, no matter how many times he told me. It didn't matter, though. The metal modifications felt amazing whether or not I knew what to call them.

"Like what you see?" Nixon asked with a smirk.

Of course I did. We both knew how much I loved to suck him off. No one fell apart while receiving head the way Nixon did. I loved the way his head would fall back as he moaned my name, or the drunk look in his eyes while he watched me.

I bit my lip, my hands trailing down my body to relieve some of the pressure building inside me. Maybe I did have some time to play...

Damn it, Poppy! Focus!

Turning away, I grabbed the towel off my head and tossed it aside. If I didn't look at his stupidly sexy body, I could pretend he wasn't there. Except he was there.

I didn't need to see Nixon to know he was looking at me like a dog looks at a steak. Over a decade of friendship and cohabitating meant we were in tune with each other's thoughts. That's why I knew he was still watching, waiting for me to give in. That's also why he knew how close I was to jumping on the bed and joining him, no matter how hard I pretended I wasn't.

My heart raced as I slowly lost the internal war waging inside of me. My clit ached to be touched, and there was a gorgeous man on my bed who would be more than willing to lend a helping hand. Or tongue. Or cock. All I had to do was join him on the bed.

Focus, Poppy. You can't have a dick inside you when the oven timer goes off. I mean, I could. I would just have to hop off long enough to grab the food...

That wouldn't work. I needed to prep the next dish so it could go in as soon as the cornbread dressing was done. As much as I wanted to, now wasn't the time.

"Quit fooling around," I huffed as I ran my fingers through my damp hair. I needed to focus on something else, anything else.

Relief washed over me as I heard him shuffle off the bed, followed by a small twinge of guilt. It was Thanksgiving, and while that may not mean much to most, it meant a lot to me. It was a time for feasting and friends, and here I was giving my best friend the brush off. He didn't deserve that.

Turning around to apologize and make nice, I gasped when Nixon's face was only a few inches from mine. I tried to take a step back, but he reached out and wrapped his hand around my throat. His hold was tight enough to keep me in place, but still loose enough that I could breathe.

I was trapped, at his mercy, unable to stop him from doing whatever he wanted. Fuck, was it hot!

"Cheater," I whispered.

The fucker knew I was a goner for a good hand necklace. Something about a powerful hand wrapped around my throat like a collar made me weak in the knees.

Nixon's lips curled into a dark smile as he squeezed a little tighter. *Fuck.* I whimpered, reaching out for support as my knees buckled. My nails dug into his shoulders as I tried to keep standing.

Taking advantage of my struggle, he shoved his other hand between my thighs, cupping my soaked pussy.

The little voice in my head begged me to stand my ground, but it was barely more than a whisper. Nixon's palm was warm and felt like heaven when I rubbed my clit against it. Screw standing my ground. Screw the food. I needed to release the pent up tension growing inside me.

"Such a little liar. Look how wet you are, and grinding against my hand like a little bitch in heat," he taunted me.

I whimpered again in response, melting at his dirty words. Light degradation wasn't normally my thing, but I seemed to love a lot of things with Nixon that weren't *my thing*.

Maybe it was our deep friendship, or maybe it was our undeniable chemistry. The why didn't matter in the end. The only thing that did was that Nixon had me dripping with need.

"I'm done playing games, Pops. I. Need. To. Fuck. So, you're going to get on all fours and let me fill that tight little pussy with my cum. Okay?"

There was desperation in his voice. He was barely holding on like the time he couldn't wait, and we fucked on the living room floor. The sex was amazing, but the carpet burn on my back not so much.

I swallowed and nodded in understanding, both difficult tasks with a hand around your throat.

Nixon released me, motioning toward the bed with his head. Excited, I scrambled into position, shaking my ass in the air like an excited puppy. When I looked back over my shoulder, he shook his head and motioned toward my vanity across from the foot of my bed.

The mirror.

My heart sank a little. He wanted to watch my face and make sure I kept my eyes open. He needed to know I wasn't thinking of anybody else. *Stupid fucking Cherry.*

I hated looking at myself during sex. Seeing my reflection was a huge distraction. I spent more time watching myself and critiquing my performance than I did getting lost in the moment.

Unfortunately, Nixon's ex left some wounds that hadn't quite healed yet. If he needed reassurance, then I could suck it up and give it to him. I would give him anything. All he had to do was ask.

Repositioning myself, I moved to the edge of the bed. My fingers dug into the comforter as I sucked in a breath and steadied myself. The bed dipped behind me as Nixon climbed on.

I raised my eyes to the mirror and watched his reflection. If I kept my focus on him, I could ignore my image in the reflective glass entirely. He stared at my body with hunger, licking his lips and stroking his cock as he drew closer. That was good. I could work with that.

Nixon grabbed my hips and manhandled me into the position he desired. My heart raced as he grabbed his cock and lined it at my entrance. Where was the foreplay? Yes, I was wet, but I needed more than that to be aroused enough to take him. I needed to be stretched thoroughly before he could stick it in me. We learned the hard way the first few times we hooked up what happened without preparation.

"Wait," I squeaked out as he pressed in.

"I've been waiting all morning, Pops. No more. Be a good girl and watch me fuck you in the mirror." I hated how his forceful tone made me want to shut up and obey.

"But—" I tried to argue, but the sharp sting of Nixon's palm spanking my ass rendered me speechless.

"No talking unless you're screaming my name," he growled before slowly pushing in.

Chapter 3

Punishment with Pleasure

Nixon

Was I being an asshole fucking Poppy with no prep or lube? Yes. Did I feel bad? No. *Liar.* Fine, yes. I hated hurting her. Even when she wanted a sadist in bed, I tried to be as careful and intentional with everything as possible. I couldn't completely lose myself in the moment with reckless abandonment like she did without risking the well-being of one, if not both, of us.

I slowly slid my cock into her tight little pussy, fighting the urge to slam all the way in one thrust. It was tempting after the way she treated me, but I couldn't risk causing any real damage.

About a third of the way in, I stilled so she could acclimate to the stretch. Her expression in the mirror was tight, and her whole body was stiff. I'd never be able to enjoy myself if she didn't relax.

Good luck getting Poppy to relax on Thanksgiving.

Last night, she was stressed out of her mind, which was par for the course for Thanksgiving Eve. Poppy always bit off more than she could chew around the holidays. It was part of the routine, as was me stepping in and rescuing her from herself. *Not that she seemed to care.*

Not that I thought she owed me anything for my efforts. I did everything I did out of love, but a little appreciation would have been nice.

After the prep was done, she was still buzzing with energy. I knew Poppy well enough to know she wouldn't have gotten any sleep without intervention, so I did what any good friend would do. I dragged her to my bed, parted her thighs, and had her sweet pussy for a late-night snack.

The quickest way to make Poppy chill was to make her come, but she needed to be more than just chill. After about a half hour of edging her, I finally let her come. The orgasm that tore through her body had her shaking as tears of relief streamed down her face. It was a beautiful sight even if my view had been partially obstructed.

When she finally came down from the high, I wrapped her in my arms and whispered how beautiful she was until she fell asleep. It only took a minute before she was out cold, snoring like an angel.

It hurt when I woke this morning to find my bed empty. While I had a reputation for being *friendly* when I drank, I wasn't the kind of person to have casual sex or one-night stands. Sex was an intimate experience. I needed a connection. I needed to know I wouldn't wake up the next morning alone.

When I first moved in with Poppy, she saw firsthand how I struggled with the superficial connection of a one-night stand. The soul crushing loneliness was amplified by the fact that I had just gotten out of a two-year relationship. It was during that dark time that Poppy went from a casual friend to one of the most important people in my life.

When I woke up and found the bed empty, I knew she was probably in the kitchen, hard at work. That didn't stop cold, dark feelings from creeping in. She knew better. We had our special arrangement for a reason.

All I needed was a moment of her time to recenter myself, but she brushed me off at every attempt. *This is a stressful time of year for her*, I tried to remind myself. That was of little consolation when I felt used and unseen. If I didn't work through everything I was feeling and blow off some steam, I was likely to explode.

Poppy whimpered in a mix of pleasure and pain as I slid in a little further. Her face contorted between the two sensations in the mirror as she struggled to take me.

"Eyes on me," I commanded, slapping her ass with the palm of my hand.

Obediently, her eyes found mine in the mirror, giving me the undivided attention I craved. Now she couldn't ignore me, not with my cock stretching her cunt. She was mine until I said otherwise.

Without proper foreplay, I was going to have to ease my way into her. Cautiously, I began to move in slow, shallow thrusts. Poppy was tight, very tight, which made it hard to keep control. Her pussy felt like a heavenly vise squeezing my cock, begging me to fill her with my cum.

With every thrust in, I pushed a little deeper. Stretching her this way was a practice in patience. All I wanted to do was fuck her like a feral animal until she was screaming my name, but I couldn't without risking real damage to Poppy. I'd never forgive myself if I put her through hell, even when mad.

Marathon, not a sprint. Marathon, not a sprint. The words replayed in my head over and over as I fought for control. It didn't help that Poppy was making the lewdest goddamn noises in response to my every thrust, like a goddamn porn star.

"Please, Nixon! Harder! Faster!" she begged, dipping her head and raising her ass to force me deeper.

Damn fucking Poppy, always trying to take control.

I grabbed her damp hair, twisting it around my hand so she couldn't escape, and pulled hard. Her head yanked upward, our eyes meeting in the mirror. With anyone else, I would have been worried about hurting them, but this was Poppy. With a flushed face and blown-out pupils, she looked like she was blissed out of her mind with arousal.

"So fucking greedy. You'll get what I give you and you'll thank me for it like a good little slut, won't you?" I growled.

Poppy tried to nod, but whimpered when she felt the resistance from my hold on her hair. She tried again, the walls of her cunt squeezing me as she whimpered in pain. She was such a fucking masochist sometimes, and it drove me wild.

Be the responsible one.

"Words, Poppy," I ordered through gritted teeth. "Use your fucking words."

Marathon, not a sprint. Marathon, not a sprint.

I was hanging on by the thinnest of threads. Her sweet whimpers called out to the sadist in me, begging me to let loose.

She'll be sore after. You don't want to really hurt her.

And then it happened. That clever little brat knew exactly what strings to pull to get her little puppet to perform. Poppy looked me dead in the eyes through the mirror and said the magic words.

"Yes, sir."

"Yes, you fucking will," I growled in response.

I shouldn't. I knew I shouldn't, but those two words always did me in. Once the floodgates opened, all my built-up frustration poured out of me.

I fucked Poppy hard, like she was mine, because in that moment she *was* mine. Mine to punish. Mine to claim. Mine.

She tried to bury her face in the bed and muffle her sweet cries of ecstasy, but I wouldn't let her. With one hand on her hip, the other kept a tight hold on her hair while I rammed into her cunt over and over. Poppy would not deny me the tortured pleasure that painted her face as I overwhelmed her senses.

Watching her writhe in pleasure in the reflective glass was too much. I couldn't stop the orgasm barreling through me, no matter how badly I wanted to prolong our moment of heaven.

I came with a howl, coming inside her as I drowned in euphoria. The powerful orgasm consumed me until there was nothing left but me and her.

Awareness slowly returned as I came down from the high.

"Palomino, mother fucker! Palomino!" Poppy shrieked.

The post nut glow vanished as panic hit me like a brick wall. Palomino was our safe word.

"Fuck!" I shouted, pulling my hands from her body. "Fuck! I—I'm sorry! What did I do?"

Nausea swept over me. *This is why we don't lose control.* I had no idea what I did or how long she had been saying the word. God, I was so fucking careless and stupid.

"Yeah, yeah. I'm fine," Poppy said, rubbing her scalp. "I just needed you to let go. You yanked a little too hard when you came."

She was fine, which was a relief, but I still felt like shit.

"I'm sorry, Pops," I said as I carefully pulled out.

Poppy only waved me off as her body slumped to the bed. "Whatever. It's fine. Just hand me a towel. I don't want your splooge on my comforter."

Reluctantly, I shuffled off the bed and grabbed the discarded towel sitting on the floor. After handing it to Poppy, I crouched next to the foot of the bed and watched her clean up. All I wanted to do was hold her and make sure she was okay, but it was clear Poppy needed a moment of space.

"Don't," she warned without looking at me.

"Don't what?" I asked, confused.

"Don't stare at me with those sad fucking puppy dog eyes after you pulled my hair and distracted me from the kitchen," she said.

Guilt punched me in the stomach. It wasn't like me to lose control when I was the one in charge.

"I said I was sorry!"

"I don't want you to be sorry. I want you to stop with the puppy dog eyes," she shot back.

"Fine," I grumbled as I dropped my eyes to the floor.

What did she want from me? And why was I the bad guy? All I wanted was to make sure she was okay. Why couldn't she let me?

After a few seconds, Poppy patted the space next to her. I looked up, curious but not willing to get my hopes up.

"Come on, Nixy-poo. I can give you a few minutes of cuddles and kisses, but then I *have* to get back to the kitchen. We have food in the oven."

I lit up like a Christmas tree, jumping next to her on the bed. The moment my arms wrapped around her everything was better. I held her close, enjoying the warmth of her skin. This right here, this was how it was supposed to be.

Chapter 4

Meddling Friends

Poppy

*K*nock. *Knock. Knock.*

I took a quick glance at the clock on the microwave as I placed the piping hot sweet potato casserole on the cooling rack. Eleven on the dot, which meant the knocking at the door was Jack and Sophie. *Right on time.*

"Nixon, grab the door!" I shouted at the top of my lungs.

I hadn't seen him since I shooed him out of my bathroom so I could put on my makeup in peace. He loved to watch the process, but I thought it was weird and it always made me uncomfortably self-conscious.

It wasn't usually so hard to get him to listen when I wanted space, but he had been extra clingy all morning. The sex and cuddles should have been enough to pacify him, but hearing our safe word undid it all. I wasn't one to use the word lightly, but the fucker was really hurting my scalp at the end.

Unfortunately, I use the word so little that hearing it triggers Nixon into full panic mode. I thought he understood I was fine when he gave me a little space right after, but the whole time we cuddled, he kept asking if I was okay. Then he wouldn't leave my side, which was whatever, but he kept getting underfoot.

I finally lost my patience when he sat down on the toilet and silently stared at me while I painted my face. I was so pissed off that I didn't care that he seemed hurt. We had so few boundaries between us it drove me crazy when he crossed one.

That was the only child in Nixon. He wasn't used to boundaries, and he didn't understand how sacred private space was. Meanwhile, I was the second oldest of five. Though the younger three saw me as more of a big sister than Amy because of the massive age gap between us and her. I could explain my views until I was blue in the face, but Nixon never truly got it because he never lived through what I did.

After I snapped, he sulked his way out of my room, and I hadn't seen him since. That was two hours ago. *Whatever.* He was probably hiding in his room, playing video games while he licked his wounds.

Another knock.

Damn it, Nixon!

He probably had his gaming headset on, which meant I could scream all day, and he would never hear me. *Must be nice to relax on Thanksgiving.*

I threw the green bean casserole in the oven, taking out my frustrations on the door as I slammed it shut. This was not the day for us to have a spat. I wouldn't last. Our little sex break already put me behind.

"Nixon Aiden Collins!" I screamed out as I stomped my way to answer the door. That ass was going to get an earful later for making me do everything by myself.

Taking a moment to compose myself, I sucked in a calming breath, holding it before letting it out. I then smoothed down the apron I had on over my dress and plastered a big smile on my face.

It's Thanksgiving, a magical time of friendship, family, and food. Except my family was in Florida. I left them all behind to follow Nixon. I missed my family...

Shaking the melancholy thoughts from my head, I readjusted my smile and opened the door.

Jack and Sophie stood on the stoop, arms full of bags and awkward smiles on their faces. *Great. Just great.*

"Happy Thanksgiving!" I greeted them cheerfully.

"Happy Thanksgiving!" Sophie said, stepping over the threshold.

Leaning in, I gave her an awkward hug before taking some of the bags. Most people brought one dish, or drinks, or extra paper plates and the like. Jack and Sophie always brought a little of everything, coming early to help set up.

"Did I hear Mommy pull out the full name? What on earth did my man do?" Jack asked with a smirk.

"More like what he isn't doing," I replied.

He gave me a knowing look, shaking his head and laughing like my frustration was the funniest thing in the world. Then again, it probably was, knowing Jack.

"Ah. Well, I'll fix that after we put these bags down," he said before leaning in and giving me a peck on the cheek, "And Happy Thanksgiving, Pops."

Only two people regularly called me Pops, Nixon and Jack. There was a lot the two of them shared. They had been friends since preschool and were more like brothers. In fact, Jack was probably the only person closer to Nixon than me.

I led the happy couple to the kitchen to unload things, not that they didn't know where it was. Jack and Sophie were over at least once a week for some reason or another. There was a time when I worried them tying the knot would mean we would see less of them, but the reverse ended up being true.

"I'll leave you ladies to it," Jack said after setting down his bags. "I'm going to find Nixon and get his help setting up the tables and stuff."

Sophie gave her husband an adorable kiss on the lips before shooing him out of the kitchen so we could have girl talk. It was our Thanksgiving tradition to pop open a bottle, or two, of wine and pregame while we finished up the food.

"You have a good man," I said as soon as he left the room.

She smiled like a giddy schoolgirl, giving me a wink as she pulled out a bottle of wine.

"I do," Sophie agreed, "but so do you."

Ah, this again.

I watched as she opened the bottle and poured us each a glass, knowing what conversation was coming. She was obsessed with pairing Nixon and me together. I think deep down she loved the idea of two friends marrying two friends and making some weird happy couple of couples. Hell, she'd probably been dreaming of it before we even met the boys.

I'd known Sophie since I was nineteen. We were both newbie cosplayers who met on an online message board for the Florida cosplay community. The whole thing was rather bizarre, looking back. We talked online for three months through the message board and AOL chat before finally meeting in person at a convention. I had no idea what a lifelong friend she would become.

Not that the others in our group weren't special at the time, but there was something different about Sophie and me. We seemed to click on a level I never had with another girl before. She was never weird or judgemental when I started to explore my sexuality. In fact, she was one of the few people who seemed understanding that I didn't want to label myself anything one way or another until I was sure.

Two years later, we met Jack and Nixon. Our cosplay group was dressed as the Sailor Scouts from Sailor Moon. I was Sailor Jupiter, and Sophie was Sailor Moon. Some creep was apparently following us around the con, trying to get up-skirt shots. We only found out because some guy dressed up as Spider-Man started making a scene, shaming the guy and forcing him to delete the pictures.

Taking the glass of wine from Sophie, I took a slow sip before replying.

"Nixon and I aren't like that. We're close, but he doesn't see me *that* way. We're just best friends that fuck around sometimes."

Sophie started laughing. "I love you Poppy, but you're an idiot. That boy has had eyes for you since the day he met you."

"Sure," I said sarcastically. "That's why he started dating Ginny two weeks later."

Ginny was the Sailor Mars in our group. From the moment the friendly neighborhood Spider-Man removed his mask and introduced himself, Ginny was smitten, throwing herself all over him.

The smile dropped from Sophie's face as she gave me a look that silently said "bless your heart."

"Sweetheart, you were the one he was protecting from that creep at the con. You know that, right? It was like he was shielding you from the pervert. And then he never left your side that first day. He only started dating Ginny because she threw herself at him like a bitch in heat, and you barely acknowledged him."

It was sweet how she remembered things, it really was, but I couldn't help feeling like she remembered that day how she wanted to. Then again, I didn't remember much past the initial meeting and the way Ginny hung all over him.

At that point in time, Ginny was one of my closest friends. If she had her sights set on a guy that wasn't on my immediate radar, then I wouldn't go out of my way to notice him like that. I didn't realize what kind of catch Nixon was until a few months later, but by then he was in an established relationship with Ginny, planning to move down to Florida to be with her.

"Well, it doesn't matter now," I said with a sigh.

"True. You are the one living with him, and Ginny is newly divorced," Sophie said with a smirk.

"Really?" I asked, surprised. Though, I wasn't *that* surprised.

Nixon and I weren't particularly close when Ginny dumped him. We were friends; we hung out in all the same circles, but never just the two of us. So imagine my surprise when Nixon showed up on my door with eyes red from crying, looking for a couch to sleep on.

Ginny threw him out after she dumped him. He hadn't even done anything wrong. She was just over the relationship and wanted him out ASAP so she could move on with her life. That bitchy move alone was enough to piss me off, but then he shared things about their relationship that first night, and it broke my heart.

It wasn't even like he was trying to trash Ginny. The poor guy was in shock, trying to process a breakup that, in his eyes, came out of nowhere. That night I learned what an overly nice people pleaser Nixon could be, and I swore to protect his soft heart.

The crazy thing was, I wasn't the one to end the friendship between me and Ginny. Apparently, giving Nixon a couch to crash on so he wasn't sleeping on the streets wasn't being supportive of Ginny and her new direction in life. According to her, a real friend would have slammed the door in his face.

"Yep," Sophie said, giving me a look as she took a sip of her wine.

"What happened?" I pressed. A sick part of me wanted to hear she was abandoned, and her heart shattered in a million pieces.

Sophie shrugged, "Ginny being Ginny."

That got a chuckle out of me. Ginny being Ginny was a running joke amongst the old crew. Most dropped contact after she blew up at me. A few still kept in touch, like Sophie, but the contacts were few and far between. Honestly, I was surprised they still talked since I knew Jack hated Ginny to the point that he wouldn't let Sophie invite her to the wedding.

"But that's not the point," Sophie continued. "You and Nixon are meant to be."

"No," I said, shaking my head, "I'm too selfish. We both know how I can get. Nixon is sweet. He deserves someone better."

When it came to lovers, I had a short attention span. I rarely dated someone for over six months, and I used to thrive on one-night stands. Every encounter was shiny and new with no strings. Well, I considered myself thriving. Sophie and Nixon referred to that period of my life as reckless. And that was my point. Nixon and I were great lovers and even better friends, but that didn't mean we would be compatible in a relationship.

"Fine," Sophie said, frowning.

It was obvious the conversation was far from over, but at least she seemed willing to drop it for now.

Chapter 5

Hard Truths are Easy to Ignore

Nixon

F reshly showered with a towel around my waist, I entered my bedroom to find Jack waiting. He leaned back in my gaming chair, watching me cross the room to my dresser with the biggest, shit-eating grin plastered on his face. That was never a good sign.

"She was yelling for you, Nixon Aiden Collins," he teased.

Fuck. That really wasn't a good sign. And why was the asshole smiling about it?

"I was in the shower with the music blaring," I said, as if he was the one I needed to explain myself to.

Poppy must have been pissed if she was screaming my full name. I doubt she would believe the running water and music drowned her out even if it was the truth.

"Uh huh," Jack said with the same stupid grin. *Ass.*

"Whatever." I huffed, marching to my dresser and pulling out a pair of novelty Thanksgiving boxer briefs Poppy bought me a few years back.

I had a whole collection of goofy clothing based on various holidays that were gifts from Poppy. Some pieces, like my many ugly Christmas sweaters, she bought while other pieces, like the bow tie with miniature turkeys on it, she made.

Slipping on the underwear under my towel, I let out a sigh. Jack said nothing, patiently waiting for me to unload.

"She wanted space, so I was giving her space," I explained.

"I get it, man. You were just doing what she asked. We're not mind readers," he said, holding up his hands in defense.

He didn't get it. Not that Sophie and he never fought, they just never fought about the same things as Poppy and me. Our relationships were very different.

"Is she that mad?" I asked, despite already knowing the answer.

"Eh? She's Poppy on Thanksgiving," he said, shrugging.

I ran a hand down my face as I let out another frustrated sigh. Everyone else saw Poppy as the perfect Thanksgiving hostess, but a few of us closest to her knew the truth. The Friendsgiving potluck, filling the house with more and more people each year, was all a coping mechanism.

Dropping the towel and grabbing my skinny jeans, I stared at the ground as I slipped them on.

"She misses her family," I explained.

Now it was Jack's turn to let out a pensive sigh. "Why don't you drag her home one year? Her family loves you, right?"

It wasn't that easy. Yes, her family loved me. They welcomed me with open arms to every family event like I was one of them. Even after Poppy followed me up north, they still loved me. Her mom and I had weekly talks on the phone. The problem wasn't her family. It was her.

"I tried. She doesn't want to abandon everyone here," I said, throwing my arms in the air in defeat.

The excuses never ended. She couldn't leave me alone during the holidays even if I was in a relationship.

"Last year, I suggested she should go. I even said I'd go with her. Nope. She couldn't risk any of our usual guests not having somewhere to go," I continued to explain. There was always a reason.

"That's just an excuse," Jack said.

"No shit, Sherlock. But I'm not going to call her on it. You know how defensive she can get."

We both went silent. There was no offering a solution when Poppy already had one. She threw herself into making this time of year amazing for everyone else, and I did what I could to make it amazing for her.

After putting on my shirt, I stepped over to the small mirror I kept on my dresser.

"A bowtie with jeans? Really, Nixon?" Jack asked.

"It will cheer her up to see me wear it. You think I don't know how to get out of the doghouse," I said with a smirk.

Turning around, Jack wasn't laughing.

"For some reason, I thought you two would be on cloud nine when I arrived. I remember the last Thanksgiving that you were both single. You were so cuddly and in love. I thought for sure—"

"She doesn't feel that way," I said before he could finish.

"You know that's not true, Nixon," he replied.

"You're right," I snapped, "I know it's not true! You know it's not true! Sophie knows it's not true! But Poppy? She has no idea how she really feels. Or maybe she does, but she's still too fucking scared of commitment. So for the sake of our friendship and my own sanity, I force myself to believe the lie."

My chest rose and fell with every breath as I tried to remain calm. This was not a conversation I wanted to have.

Jack sighed as he leaned forward in my chair. He looked like a doctor who was about to tell their patient that their condition was terminal.

"This codependency isn't healthy. Soph will kill me for saying this, but maybe you two need some space."

And there it was.

"No," I said, shaking my head, "it's not that bad. If she's happy, then I'm happy. Even when it's with someone else."

And it was true. I wouldn't have survived if I didn't mean every word. Our attraction ebbed and flowed over the years. Sometimes we were in sync, sometimes not, but I could honestly say that I was happiest when she was happy, whether it was with me or not.

"Fine. I'll let it go. I just don't get how you can be happy when she's with someone else," he said, shaking his head.

"Really? That's rich coming from the guy with a cuckolding fetish," I scoffed.

Jack fidgeted uncomfortably in the chair, no longer able to look me in the eye. It was a low blow, but his judgemental attitude was pissing me off. I'd fucked Sophie plenty of times at his request while he watched , and not once did I judge him for it.

"That's different," he mumbled.

I felt like shit. *Because you aren't the aggressive type.* Nope, that was Poppy, and she would destroy Jack if she caught even the slightest whiff of us fighting.

"Fuck," I said after a long silence, "I don't want to fight. And I don't care if you enjoy watching people fuck your wife. Just trust I know what's good for me?"

Jack raised his head and flashed me a half-hearted smile. "You're right. Sorry."

"I'm going to tell Sophie you think Poppy and I need a break. It's going to destroy her dream of neighboring cottages or whatever," I teased, trying to lighten the mood.

"Don't you dare. She'll have my balls!" Jack said as he leapt from the chair.

He wasn't wrong. She probably would.

Chapter 6

But I Don't Want Space

Nixon

I t was a quarter till eleven and set up was finally done. Guests were trickling in, and I was hiding in my room so I could get my head on straight. It wasn't like me to avoid a crowd, especially when I was the host, but there was a pain in my chest that would not go away. The dull ache clouded my thoughts, making it hard to smile and pretend everything was okay.

The conversation with Jack got under my skin more than I wanted to admit. I had been living with Poppy for fourteen years. Fourteen years! That was over a third of my life. I could barely remember how I lived without her, and Jack thought we needed space. Did he even know me?

There was a time when I would have trusted his wisdom without question, but things were different now compared to when we were kids. We both changed a lot over the years, and those changes colored how we saw the world around us.

The thought of separating from my partner-in-life left a bitter taste in my mouth. Jack meant well, I'm sure, but he had no idea what he was talking about. To him, a wedding ring on that special someone's finger was the end goal. It was one of the few influences of our upbringing that followed him into adulthood.

That was where we differed. I left that all behind when my family cut me off. Love didn't need a ring, not that I wouldn't drop to one knee in an instant if that's what I thought Poppy truly wanted, but she didn't and I was okay with that.

Jack probably thought I spent everyday wasting away as I hopelessly pined after her. That couldn't be further from the truth. Yes, sometimes my very soul ached to be with her, but I never let that stop me from living. I went on dates. I had meaningful relationships.

Only because she forces you to. True, but that's why we worked so well. Poppy was there for me at my lowest points. She would let me sulk and cry, she would hold and comfort me, and then she'd force me to pick myself up and move on. Without her, I would be lost. Why couldn't Jack see that?

Tap. Tap. Tap.

My heart jumped at the unexpected rapping on my bedroom door. Someone must have noticed I was MIA from the party. *Crap.*

"Nixy?" Poppy called.

My heart simultaneously cried out in joy and pain at the sound of her voice. This wasn't good. I couldn't let Poppy see me like this.

"Yeah. In here, give me a second," I replied.

My chest felt tight, like my rib cage was constricting my lungs. Was that a thing that could happen?

Crouching down into a squat, I held my head and tried to focus on my breathing. If I could calm down, I would be fine. *Stupid fucking Jack.*

The door creaked open and then clicked shut. I didn't have to look to know Poppy was leaning against the door, watching me. I could smell the autumn spiced perfume she loved so much this time of year. It wafted through the room, making my mouth water.

"What's wrong?" The concern in her voice tore my heart. Of course she was concerned. Who wouldn't be seeing me in such a state?

Standing, I brushed my hands down my shirt and adjusted my glasses, pretending she didn't just catch me in crisis mode.

"Nothing," I replied.

Poppy tilted her head and studied me. She saw right through me, and I knew it. My stomach twisted in knots as I waited for her to say something, anything.

"Nixon," she said softly, taking a step forward.

"I'm fine, Pops. Really." I flashed a tight smile, hoping she would drop it.

Poppy wasn't having it. She walked right to me and placed her hand on my chest, over my heart. I could feel her warmth through the fabric of my cotton shirt. The small action felt intimate and almost suffocating.

"Talk to me." Her voice was barely more than a whisper, yet it felt deafening.

"Jack and I had a disagreement. It's nothing," I said, cursing myself the moment the words left my lips.

Poppy didn't say anything. She lifted her other hand to my cheek and guided me toward her. I leaned down, following her lead, letting her lips brush against mine. The sensation was electric. Goosebumps rose all over my skin.

The kiss was a chaste tease at best, but the hold it had on me was insane. My mouth went dry, the need for more overwhelming me.

"Poppy," I whimpered.

I could feel her smile against my lips. She loved to torture and tease me as much as she loved for me to take control.

Gathering a fistful of my shirt, she held me close as our lips crashed together in a fiery passion that made my cock ache.

Fireworks exploded around us as her tongue forced its way inside me. She was fierce and possessive in her efforts to claim me with a force that left my knees weak.

The world around us vanished. My senses fried. The only thing my mind could comprehend was Poppy. I was putty to be molded into whatever form she wished.

When we broke for air, my head was spinning. It took a few minutes for the world to come back into focus. Somehow we had ended up on my bed, lying side by side. *When did we move?*

Poppy stared into my eyes, holding me captive in ways she could never possibly understand. Reaching out, I brushed a lock of her soft, brown hair behind her ear. The moment between us was perfect.

"What did you argue about?" she asked, breaking the moment.

I turned away, staring at the ceiling instead of acknowledging her question. Unwilling to back down, Poppy climbed on top and straddled my hips. When I still wouldn't look at her, she grabbed my face and forced me to comply.

"It doesn't matter," I replied.

My heart raced as I silently prayed for her to let it go. If we didn't talk about it, then nothing would happen and we would be safe.

Poppy's thumb trailed over my bottom lip, and she watched me while contemplating her next move. I didn't know why I was trying to delay the inevitable. We both knew she could make me talk if she really wanted to.

"You're hurting, Nixy. You know how much it hurts me when you're in pain."

That was such a low fucking blow, but a smart move on her part. I knew she was manipulating me, but I couldn't bear the idea that I was causing her pain.

Needing to feel closer to her, I reached under the skirt of her dress and placed my hands on her thighs. Her warm, soft skin gave me comfort.

"Do you ever wish you had space from me? Like maybe we shouldn't live together?" My voice cracked as I forced the words out. The question felt wrong.

Poppy froze. Panic settled in my gut as her face morphed into something between hurt and anger. This was it, the beginning of the end.

"What? Why? Is this because I didn't want you in the bathroom earlier? We've been over this. It's natural to want a few minutes alone here and there. That doesn't mean I don't want you as a roommate anymore."

The knot in my stomach tightened as I realized she misunderstood the question. My fingers dug into her thighs as I tried to better ask the question.

"That—that's not what I mean. Do you think we're codependent?" I asked, holding my breath.

"Duh?"

Duh? That wasn't the response I expected. I stared back, blinking, unsure what to say.

Poppy rolled her eyes and sighed, clearly annoyed, and I had no idea why.

"I don't think you understand what—"

She held a finger to my lips, shushing me.

"Do you remember what condition I was living in when you first crashed on my couch?"

I winced. Her place was a mess. The dishes hadn't been done in a week or two, and trash bags were piled by the front door. I didn't understand at the time how someone could have the energy to change the bags, but not take them to the dumpster.

Poppy was crazy outgoing, but her batteries deeply relied on interactions with other people. If she went too long without social contact, then she started to shut down. Basic tasks became a struggle, as well as making plans with others, which only exacerbated the issue. It was a hard cycle to break once she was in it.

"Exactly. Our parasitic friendship is the only reason I don't hide from the world for weeks at a time, unable to find the motivation to do anything more than order takeout," she explained.

Using the word parasitic aside, it felt good to hear Poppy say she needed me. Not a warm body, me.

A smile crossed my lips as the tension drained away.

"There he is," she said, smiling back.

With her hands planted on either side of my head, Poppy leaned closer until her face was hovering just above mine.

"I'm going to kill him." The look on her face left no doubt in her statement. Poppy was going to march out there and dress Jack down in front of everyone.

I wrapped my arms around her waist, trapping her against my body. The last thing I needed was my two best friends fighting. *And the secrets he might spill in retaliation.*

"Don't, please. It's Thanksgiving," I pleaded. It was a lame excuse, but I was desperate.

"But you're upset—"

"Then make me feel better!" I blurted out without thinking.

The devilish grin that crossed her lips made me wish I put some thought into my words before speaking.

Poppy placed her hands on my chest and pushed up, breaking from my hold. I swallowed the lump in my throat as I stared up at her, waiting to see what she had in store.

"Touch me," she commanded.

Chapter 7

Touch Me Like You Mean It

Nixon

"What?" I asked, convinced I misheard her.

Poppy straightened her back, casting down a frightening glare in my direction. I shriveled a little inside, fearing I somehow made things worse.

"I said touch me. It's not that hard to understand, Nixon. You fucked me without any foreplay earlier. You owe me an O." The accusation stung as much as her sharp tone. Why was she being brash with me?

I should have argued that I didn't owe her shit. Our session earlier set the scales back to zero after I spent the night before edging her and getting nothing in return. As far as I was concerned, we were even.

And yet my hand moved up her thigh, any thought of resistance fading away the higher I reached. I wasn't a prideful person who would deny themselves something they loved to prove a point.

(*Cough* *Cough* Poppy) I loved any excuse to touch her. Even the smallest caress against her skin would give me a serotonin boost that would last for hours.

The scowl on Poppy's face dropped, a small smile peeking through to reward my compliance. She was pleased, which eased some of the growing tension inside me.

My hand traveled until I reached the apex of her thighs. Those beautiful brown eyes watched me, waiting to see what I would do next. *Everything you ever wanted*, I thought, wishing she could read my mind.

My dick twitched at the soft gasp that fell from Poppy's lips as my knuckles lightly grazed over her cotton panties. I slipped my hand inside the fabric, groaning from the feel of her heat. My cock ached, desperate to trade places with my hand, but I couldn't.

Poppy closed her eyes and threw her head back, releasing the lewdest moan as I slid a single finger between her wet folds and breached her entrance. There was nothing quiet about her reaction. Any guests walking near my room surely heard her.

Good. Let them hear. Let them know who makes her feel like this.

My thumb circled her clit while I pumped a single finger inside her. She wriggled and writhed, rewarding me with more sounds of pleasure in response. It was a beautifully captivating show that I couldn't take my eyes off of.

"Another finger, Nixon," she whimpered.

I was quick to obey, adding another. My dick throbbed in pain, needing to feel the squeeze of her cunt the way my finger did as I stretched her. She was tight, so fucking tight.

"It feels so good when you behave," she praised me.

"Thank you," I replied, breathless and barely aware.

I continued my efforts, lost in a trance. My main focus was on the beautiful woman soaking my hand. I knew her body well. She wasn't far from completely falling apart.

Poppy grabbed my other hand, bringing the palm to her lips. Her fingers dug in, another sign she was teetering on the edge. Our eyes met, and I felt myself drowning as she lightly kissed my palm. The move was too emotional for what we were doing.

"Don't look away," she snapped when I tried to close my eyes.

Her stare held me captive as she took my pointer finger and slowly ran her tongue from base to tip. It wasn't my cock, and I couldn't come from the action, but my body didn't seem to get the memo. My breath quickened and my entire body felt too hot for my clothes.

I whimpered in response, silently begging my mistress to never release me from her hold. She took my finger into her mouth and sucked hard, moaning around the digit as I edged her closer to her climax.

"Please," I begged. What for? I had no fucking clue. There was too much going on for me to have a clear thought of my own.

"Please," I continued, repeating the word over and over.

Poppy let out a whine as the walls of her cunt spasmed around my finger. I continued my efforts, working her through her orgasm until she was limp, and no longer able to hold herself up.

An uncomfortable silence fell over the room. Poppy was flopped on my chest, sated with pleasure, but something was missing. I couldn't place what was off, but the wrongness of it was sufficient.

I lay quietly, matching my breaths to hers. It was something I did regularly in her presence when things didn't feel quite right. She was my calm in any storm.

"That was great, Nixy. You did an amazing job," she praised.

And just like that, my world was right again. I smiled brightly, proud of what I accomplished, even though I was now hard as a fucking rock.

Down boy. We will get to play later.

Poppy rolled off of me and stumbled to her feet. I made no attempt to join her as she straightened out her dress and ran her fingers through her hair.

"Lick your fingers clean," she ordered without sparing a glance in my direction.

Absent-mindedly, I brought my fingers to my lips and sucked them clean of her juices. I hummed in satisfaction as I savored the tangy taste that was unique to Poppy. She was my favorite flavor by far.

"Can I eat you later?" I asked, slightly distracted.

"And then fuck me hard after?" Poppy said with a smile. The way she could read my mind was so fucking hot.

"Yes, please," I said with excitement as I jumped off the bed. I felt like a kid on Christmas and Santa had just offered me my favorite toy.

Poppy rolled her eyes and chuckled as she shook her head. "Sure."

Something was funny, but the joke flew over my head. Whatever. I was happy enough we would get to play more later, assuming everyone left at a decent time.

I pulled Poppy in for a tight hug, hoping she didn't notice the erection that was digging into her hip. *Like she wouldn't notice that monster*. I smirked to myself.

"Do you need to take care of that?" she asked.

Was that an option?

"No, I can wait for tonight," I replied, sure that it was a test of some sort.

Poppy pulled back and gave me a look that made me second guess my answer. Was I supposed to ask her for help? No, that didn't seem right. But then why was she studying me?

"I think you deserve a reward after making me come so quickly, Nixy," she cooed seductively.

A reward? My cock loved the sound of that.

"I'm going to go take care of our guests so no one suspects anything while you take matters into your own hands. Use that video of me you think I don't know about for inspiration. The one from your birthday two years ago. I know you didn't delete it after."

I blushed from her calling me out so easily. To be fair, she never asked me to delete the video. I think she just assumed I deleted any media of her each time I entered a new relationship. On the bright side, I wouldn't have to hide my favorite spank bank video anymore.

"Of course, Poppy," I agreed eagerly, "I'll be quick and rejoin you."

"No, take your time and enjoy yourself. Then, come find me."

I must have done a great job if she was going to let me bail from hosting duties for a bit to jack off. Not that I was going to question her and risk losing the privilege. I wasn't stupid.

"Thanks, Pops," I said.

She leaned in, giving me a peck on the cheek before leaving. I quickly locked the door and grabbed my earbuds and phone, eager for a little me time.

Chapter 8

Kismet and Curses

Poppy

Exiting Nixon's room, I let out a sigh. None of that went the way I expected. I was only trying to distract him, make him forget his anxieties. Like an idiot, I didn't think twice about being firm with him. *You know what that does to him!*

Nixon didn't enter a trancelike state when he was in subspace. I'm not even sure you could call what he experienced subspace. Maybe subzone was a more appropriate term? It was like caring for a little puppy dog. He was excitable, eager to please, and loved being lavished with praise and attention. The downside was how needy and territorial he got, something I wasn't in the mood for today.

I should have known what was happening the moment he started begging unprompted, but I was too far gone myself. It wasn't until he started matching my breathing after that I realized something was up. That was a calming technique I taught him to stay centered when we played.

I threw out a command to test my theory, and I knew for certain when I told him he could masturbate. The look of pure excitement in his eyes was classic sub Nixon. Any other time, he would have given me a snarky comeback in response.

The timing couldn't have been worse. We had a house full of people that needed attention, but Nixon was going to need a bit of coddling himself if he didn't snap out of it soon.

The worst part was that I wasn't sure Nixon realized where his head was at. His feelings always seemed like they were amplified when he was in that state. Who knew how he would lash out if he started feeling things and wasn't self aware enough to know why?

Hopefully, some alone time and post nut clarity would be enough to get his head on straight. If not, I wasn't sure I could handle him and my duties as hostess.

Not your fault, I thought to myself. No, it was Jack's, but I was the one who had to clean up the mess. *Says who?*

I stood for a moment, contemplating the answer. Technically, I didn't have to clean up anyone's messes but my own. At the same time, I loved Nixon, and I did contribute to the growing disaster that was touching himself in his room.

Glancing at my smartwatch, I decided I had a little time before I needed to worry. It was Thanksgiving, and I spent a lot of time cooking and cleaning in preparation. I deserved to enjoy the fruits of my labor, damn it!

What should have been a simple task dragged out as various guests kept interrupting. Somehow, I managed to hold my smile and fill my plate while pretending to listen to what each person was saying. I felt bad that no one was getting my full attention, but I was hungry and distracted. It didn't help that I was entertaining the crowd alone, since Nixon took my suggestion to take his time seriously.

Do you really want him greeting the guests in that state, the little voice asked. The answer was no, but that didn't make things any less frustrating. If only Jack had minded his own business.

My hand tightened around the serving spoon of mashed potatoes as I fought the urge to find Jack and beat him with it. Would it ruin the celebration? Who knew? Maybe a little murder would make the event more entertaining.

"Poppy?" a familiar voice called out.

"Huh?" I had been so distracted that I didn't see Quinn, one of my friends from work, walk up.

She stared at me, tilting her head to the side with a frown. "Are you okay?"

No, I wasn't fine. I was tired, hungry, and pissed for so many reasons. Quinn knew me well enough that I could vent without judgment, but we weren't alone and I didn't want to talk about certain things when anyone could listen in.

"Yeah, I'm fine." I tried to reassure her, but she could see right through me.

"You're squeezing the serving spoon so tight that your hand is turning red," she said.

Looking down, I realized that I was, in fact, choking the life out of a spoon. *Way to go, Poppy.* As soon as I released the innocent utensil, my hand began to throb.

"Damn it," I muttered, flexing my hand to ease some of the ache.

"You seem stressed. Where's Nixon?" she pressed.

"He's around," I replied, trying to avoid the subject.

"Okay? I guess I'm just used to seeing him glued to your side, even at work."

For some reason, her comment struck a nerve. Not in a bad way, but after what Nixon said, I couldn't help reacting.

"Do you think that's a bad thing?" I asked.

Quinn shrugged. "Honestly? I don't think it's good or bad. It just is."

She got it. If only Jack could understand instead of winding Nixon up, my life would be perfect.

"There you are, Poppy! I've been looking all over for you!" My heart stilled upon hearing a smooth, masculine voice I wasn't expecting.

No, it couldn't be...

Turning toward the sound, I watched the last person I thought I would see approaching us, wearing the biggest smile. He was over six feet of sculpted muscles and tan skin with dirty blond hair and crystal blue eyes—my unobtainable crush for the last five years, Harrison.

"Um, hi. You came," I said, a bit surprised. I had extended him an invite for a few years now, but I never imagined he would actually show.

"Yes. When I didn't see you at first, I started to worry I crashed a stranger's Friendsgiving dinner. I mean, a few of these people look familiar, but it's hard to know when you are used to seeing everyone in costumes," he explained with a nervous chuckle.

"Yeah." The one word was all I could manage. My mind was still trying to catch up with the fact that he was actually here.

The universe had a strange sense of humor when it came to me and Harrison. Our meeting was a series of chance encounters that felt too outlandish to be real life.

The first time we met was at a convention. He was the Joker, and I was Harley Quinn. We took a few pictures together, had a small chat, and then went our separate ways. There was nothing particularly special about that first meeting beyond an undeniable chemistry.

A few months later, it happened again at another con. He was Captain America, and I was one of the Star Spangled Singers from the first movie. Neither of us recognized the other since our prior costumes involved fully painted faces. He caught me ogling America's Ass and made a cheeky comment. When I apologized and introduced myself, his bright blue eyes started to sparkle with excitement.

We talked for a bit and snapped a few pictures, but that was it. I had a boyfriend at the time, so it didn't feel right to ask for his information.

The third time it happened was the craziest of all. I was dressed as the fox version of Maid Marian from Disney's Robin Hood, and he was Robin Hood in the stork disguise. It blew both our minds that two strangers could be so in sync, especially considering our choices in costumes that time weren't exactly common like in the past.

After that, we exchanged contact information, but we never took it further than the occasional text outside of our convention interactions. We had great chemistry, but horrible timing since neither of us was ever single at the same time. Still, I invited him to the Friendsgiving potluck every year out of some strange hope he would show up.

Quinn cleared her throat, and it was then that I realized I had been staring like a lovesick puppy. *How embarrassing!*

"I'm going to let you two catch up," she said, departing before I could stop her.

And then there were two.

This was bad. Nixon knew about the ongoing saga that was me and Harrison. While he didn't believe the universe had some grandiose plans for me and Harrison, he always humored me and listened when I talked. But something told me Nixon wasn't in the mood to humor me today, at least not about other men.

"You look beautiful in regular clothes," Harrison said.

The way his eyes traveled over my body made me think it wasn't my clothes he was looking at. My cheeks flushed as his hungry gaze paused at my hips and breasts before returning to my face.

"So do you," I replied with a timid smile.

Lame. Lame. Lame. The little voice in my head chanted. I couldn't help it. I was off my game. Normally, I would ditch the party and drag the guy to my room for some fun, but that wasn't an option. I wasn't a free agent until January.

I might not be the kind of woman who was good enough to be with Nixon long-term, but I could keep my flirty ass in line for two measly months. If he was willing to tank his chances with Rupert, then I could resist Harrison for a little bit longer.

I took a step back, hoping some distance would strengthen my resolve. Harrison took a step forward in response. The look in his eyes said he was determined to not let me slip through his fingers this time, and a stupid part of me wanted him to succeed.

Fuck you, universe. Really and truly.

"We always have the worst timing, don't we?" I said, before things could escalate further.

"Do we?" he asked. There was still a small sliver of hope in his eyes that almost broke me.

My eyes dropped to the ground, unable to bear the look of disappointment on his face. *It's better this way*, I tried to convince myself. We'd been going back and forth for so long that I had built the idea of what could have been into something that wasn't realistic. Shooting a torpedo through the whole thing before it could finally start meant that he could never disappoint me.

"Holy shit! Is that Harrison?" Nixon asked in an over the top voice as he joined the conversation.

Fuck.

I was no stranger to Jealous Nixon and his wrath, but I had been fortunate enough to be nothing more than a spectator in the past. He masked his feelings with an overly friendly appearance and passive aggressive remarks.

We might not have been perfect with our communication, but we checked in with each other often any time we shared more than the roof over our head. We had to with the way we often blurred the lines of our friendship. If you waited for an issue to arise before you spoke up, then it was already too late. The last thing either of us wanted was to fall apart over a situation that was preventable.

Unfortunately, I hadn't prepared Nixon for the potential that Harrison would be here because it never crossed my mind that he would actually show. Not that it mattered at the end of the day. Pact or no pact, I was allowed to talk to other people. I had plenty of conversations with Harrison in the past while I was in committed relationships. There was no reason for Nixon to get bent out of shape.

"Um, hi?" Harrison said hesitantly. He gave me a questioning glance before turning his attention back to Nixon. "I'm sorry, have we met before?"

Nixon's smile grew wider, like a crazed evil villain. "No, but I've heard a lot about you. Poppy talks about you at length, so much that I feel like I already know you."

My cheeks burned with embarrassment. The jerk purposely made it sound weird. I silently pleaded with him to stop, but he wouldn't look in my direction. His attention was laser focused on Harrison.

"I'm Nixon, by the way. Welcome to my home," he said, reaching out and offering his hand.

Harrison hesitantly accepted while looking at me for an explanation.

"We're roommates," I corrected before adding, "and best friends, like Chandler and Joey."

Nixon's eye twitched, but he managed to keep his carefully crafted smile in place. He hated when I made that comparison, but I thought it was spot on.

Harrison gave me a blank look until Nixon spoke up.

"She's making a *Friends* reference," he explained.

"No, no. I got that. I'm just confused why them," Harrison clarified.

"She thinks she's Joey," he replied, rolling his eyes.

"Whatever, I totally am. Watch," I insisted.

Looking around, I spotted a small brunette walking past us. Bingo. Brooke was a sweetie, but very shy. Nixon met her at the comic shop a couple years back, and they bonded over their mutual obsession with Spider-Man.

I caught her eye, nodded in her direction and gave my best, "How you doin'?"

Brooke blushed, smiling as her eyes cast to the floor in an adorable display of bashfulness.

"H-hi, Poppy," she squeaked out, still staring at the ground. "Happy Thanksgiving."

I gave both boys a look that said *told you*. Nixon scowled, not impressed in the least by my triumphant display. Whatever. He could be sour about being wrong all he wanted.

"Happy Thanksgiving. And thank you for coming," I said, turning my attention back to Brooke.

Still red as a tomato, she nodded a quick acknowledgement and scurried to the next room.

"Like shooting fish in a barrel," I said with a smirk.

Chapter 9

A Step too Far

Nixon

"Are you done?" I asked, exasperated.

All I wanted when I walked out of my room was to find Poppy and cuddle. It was bad enough that we had a house full of people I had to get past to find her, but then I saw her talking with her stupid, cosplay, kismet crush and I saw red. How I kept it together, I had no fucking clue. Little did I know it would only get worse.

Poppy had a bad habit of bewitching my gal pals, even the straight ones. She wasn't actively trying to seduce them, but in her efforts to be welcoming, she often came on as a little more than friendly. Though, in Brooke's case, it might be on purpose.

I was ready to scold Poppy when she turned to me with her beautiful fuck-me eyes and shot out another, "How you doin'?"

A small smile tugged at the corner of my mouth as my anger vanished into thin air. I hated to admit it, but there was something magical about her impression. It was goofy, but somehow still alluring.

My dick woke right up, eager to show her how much it enjoyed her little performance despite the ample attention it received not long ago. I wanted Poppy in the worst way.

No, I needed Poppy. I needed her body under mine. I needed to feel her bare breasts against my skin while I fucked her slow and sweet. I needed to hear her scream my name while she fell apart in my arms. I needed Poppy.

She's only playing around, I tried to warn myself in some feeble attempt to protect my heart. It was no use. I was already trapped by her spell.

Then she broke it by turning to *Harrison* and delivering the line a third time. *Really, Poppy? You proved your point.*

Jealousy burned through me as he bit his lip while his eyes slowly raked over her body. She wasn't his to look at like that. She was mine. *Only for pretend.*

"Doing pretty fine," he replied, like I wasn't standing right there. *Oh, fuck this guy.*

Poppy let out a startled squeak as I grabbed her arm and pulled her towards me. There was only so much I could be expected to take, and we crossed the threshold long ago. I need to remind her of our pact and what that meant.

"Excuse us. Poppy and I need to have a little chat," I said between gritted teeth.

Harrison looked like he had something to say, but I didn't give him the chance. I dragged Poppy away at full speed, desperate to put as much space between them as possible.

"Careful! My food!" she snapped as she stumbled along.

I paused long enough to snatch the plate from her hand and placed it on the nearest empty surface. Poppy let out a frustrated growl in protest, but she would get over it. We had more pressing matters to attend to.

I needed to get Poppy alone. Whether it was to scream at her or kiss her, I hadn't decided yet.

Weaving through our guests, I ignored the snickers and passing comments about a lovers' quarrel. It was common for some of our closer friends to make jokes any time Poppy and I had a little spat. Part of me hoped Harrison would hear them gossip and lose interest.

I never liked Harrison. Something about him always rubbed me the wrong way, not that I ever said anything to Poppy. Maybe it was the way he so conveniently matched her every time they ran into each other at a con.

The first two times could have been a coincidence, but after that, it was doubtful. The more likely scenario was that he found her cosplay page on social media after the second time and stalked her online. She was always open about what costumes she was working on for which cons. *Kismet, my ass.* He wasn't good enough for her if he had to resort to lying and cheap tricks.

When we got to the room, I pulled Poppy in and slammed the door behind us. Scowling, she took a few steps back as she soothed the spot on her arm where I held her.

"What is wrong with you today?"

Was she serious? The question was almost as insulting as her behavior.

"You're flirting with every Tom, Dick, and Sally!" I shouted, throwing my hands in the air. *Emphasis on the Dick.*

I began to pace the room, using the movement to burn off some of the energy coursing through me. It wasn't like me to be so unbalanced, especially with Poppy. We had our arrangement in various forms for over a decade, with most of the kinks worked out by now. We had boundaries and rules to avoid any friendship-ruining chaos, and yet here we were.

"I wasn't flirting. I was merely demonstrating that I *am* the Joey in our relationship," she explained, then added, "don't be mad that you're Chandler."

I froze, staring at her in utter disbelief. The mental gymnastics that she was performing were gold medal worthy, I had to hand it to her.

"I don't want you flirting with other people, Pops! I want the full experience!" I demanded.

Her brow furrowed as she cocked her head to the side. "The full experience? Of what?"

"Our Holiday Pact. I want the full experience of our pact. You and me exclusive until January first," I tried to explain.

"But we are exclusive," she replied. "That's part of the pact."

This wasn't working. I needed to communicate more clearly if I was going to get through to her.

"I want to wake up each morning with you in my bed. I want to wrap my arms around you no matter who is looking. I want long, lingering stares in a crowded room. I want my lap to be your preferred seat until the end of December. And when the clock strikes midnight on the thirty-first, it's you I want to kiss."

I let out a breath, dizzy from my pseudo confession. It killed me that I was still too much a coward to say I didn't want an expiration date, but at least it was something.

I watched her, waiting for her to say something, anything, but she didn't speak. Her silence filled the room, bringing time to a crawl. The bile rose from my stomach as I realized she didn't want me. It was the very scenario I had spent the last fourteen years trying to avoid. I ruined us.

"Nixon, if we do that, then people are going to think we're in an actual relationship," she said, finally breaking her silence.

"I don't care," I told her.

"Things could get messy," she continued to argue.

"What part of our situation isn't messy, Pops? I like the messy. It's us," I replied.

"What about Rupert? I don't want—"

"I don't fucking care about Rupert! Why don't you listen to me when I talk?"

Sure, when Rupert and I first started talking, there may have been something there. I was a sucker for guys with thick muscles and very little going on up top, and the ginger rugby player fit the bill. But I never let it get very far because of the pact, and the fact that I was okay with it said volumes.

"Because I know you, probably better than you know yourself. You don't actually want to sabotage a potential relationship for something that's only temporary," she argued back.

I couldn't believe what I was hearing. It was like talking to a brick wall. There had to be a way to make her actually listen.

Chapter 10

I'll Make You Hear Me

Nixon

If words weren't working, then I had to try something else. I grabbed her by the hips, pulling her body against mine as I leaned in and kissed her. Fireworks, sparks, whatever you wanted to call it, Poppy and I had it. Every time we kissed was magic, and this time was no different. The passion between us exploded as I expressed just how badly I wanted her.

Reaching up with one hand, I tangled my fingers in her hair and tilted her head back as I deepened the kiss. She moaned in appreciation as her body melted into mine. I continued my efforts, pouring everything I couldn't say into our kiss to show her how serious I was about wanting her. She eagerly surrendered, gyrating her hips in a mindless act of desire.

If there was a heaven, this was mine. The feel of Poppy in my arms, the taste of her lips, knowing she wanted me as much as

I wanted her. If I could have stopped time, I would gladly have trapped myself in that moment forever.

When I pulled back, Poppy didn't have the love-drunk expression I had hoped for. Her brow furrowed as a frown tugged at the corners of her kiss-swollen lips, slowly chipping away at the hope that had taken root in my heart.

Something was holding her back, but what? Clearly she wanted me. The kiss was proof enough. Poppy wasn't the type to let you make out with her if she wasn't feeling it. There had to be something else going on.

Cupping her face in the palm of my hands, I tilted her head so her beautiful eyes that were so full of sadness met mine.

"Talk to me, Pops," I pleaded, barely over a whisper.

"It's just, are you sure? I don't want to sabotage your chances at happiness," she replied.

The doubt in her voice hurt my heart. How could she say such things? After everything I said and did, she still didn't believe me.

She's scared. The thought struck me, bringing with it a new sense of clarity. Of course she was scared, we both were. I was asking for a temporary deconstruction of any walls she had in place, walls that might not be easy to rebuild when the time came. The conversation had been all about me and not about her.

"My happiness or yours? Because being with you makes me happy, but I get it if I'm asking for too much. You don't have to make excuses, just be honest," I said.

Poppy took a step back, watching her hands as she ran them down the skirt of her dress as she spoke. "No, I just don't want to hear you whining come January that I scared away the possible love of your life like last time."

She looked back at me with a serious expression bordering on annoyed. I couldn't help it, the whole concept was so ridiculous that I burst out laughing.

"Love of my life? Really? He's hot. That's it. Our conversations are about—fuck, I don't even know. I've never actually listened to what he said," I replied.

Poppy huffed, unamused that I wasn't taking her fears seriously. How could I? The comparison between the two was ridiculous.

The last time we enacted the Holiday Pact things were looking like they were about to get serious for me and someone I had been pursuing. Everything got put on hold because Pops got dumped a week before Halloween. I spent that time nursing her through the worst of her heartache. I didn't mind, but come January it was like a switch flipped and she was all better. That was great for her, but my potential lover had since moved on, leaving me all alone.

"I'll live. Besides, if I had to choose between the two of you, I would choose you every single time," I continued to reassure her.

"Fine. If you say so," she said with a sigh.

She still wasn't convinced, but she wasn't actively fighting me anymore. That was a start in the right direction. Even the littlest win was enough for me at the moment. With any luck, it might grow into something more.

"Now that that's settled, can I eat?" she asked, placing a hand on her hip.

"If you're hungry, I've got something that will fill you up," I teased, trying to lighten the mood.

Poppy took another step back and raised a brow. "Really? Again? Is that even possible?"

"Eh...it's had plenty of time to rest," I said with a shrug.

The offer was obviously a joke; well, I thought it was obvious. Poppy had worked hard all day between preparing for the potluck and dealing with my shit, of course she was hungry for real food. Food that I selfishly took from her. So I was more than a little surprised when she dropped to her knees and unbuckled my belt.

"You don't have to. I was only teasing," I explained as she unzipped my pants.

"I know, but I want you to feel guilty so I can make you wait on me hand and foot later," she replied.

Knowing Poppy the way I did, there was a good chance she was being serious. The smart thing to do would have been to stop and make sure she ate, but any rational thought flew out the window when her delicate fingers wrapped around my cock.

I sucked in a breath, the coolness of her touch sending a shiver through my body. She leaned in and placed a chaste kiss on the tip of the head. The feather light brush of her lips made my eyes roll back as I let out a groan. When I opened my eyes, she was inspecting my dick like it was the most fascinating thing she had ever seen, despite the fact that she knew it better than anyone else.

"It looks like he wants to play," she teased.

"He does," I whispered in agreement. "He most definitely does."

Our little arrangement had been going on for over a decade. We shared our beds and sometimes our partners. We knew each other's bodies in a way I never thought possible before her. And yet every time she touched my cock, it felt like the first time, always new and exciting.

She smiled as she leaned in and flicked the little metal bar that pierced the head of my cock. I sucked in a sharp breath as a wave of pleasure coursed through me. Before I could recover, she wrapped her lips around my shaft, just past the frenum piercing, and hummed. The vibrations sent my body into overload, my knees almost buckling under me.

"I—I need to sit," I sputtered out.

Poppy ignored my request, switching things up. She ran her tongue up the underside of my cock, from base to tip. I shuddered with pleasure as she repeated the motion over and over, like she was licking an ice cream cone.

My fingers itched to touch her, to grab her and force myself down her throat, but I refrained. It wasn't worth the risk of blue balls if I upset her. I balled my hands into fists and forced them to my sides to fight the temptation. If Poppy wanted her fun, it was in my best interest to let her have it.

Lifting my dick slightly, she ducked down and showered my balls with attention. I bit my lips, barely stifling my groan as she began to suck one in her mouth and then the other. My legs locked into place to keep me from falling to the ground as the sensation overwhelmed me.

"Fuck, woman," I gasped.

Poppy responded by wrapping one hand around the base of my shaft, the other grabbing my thigh for support. The next thing I knew, she was giving me the sloppiest BJ I'd ever experienced.

The sweet noises of determination she made as she worked to take me deeper drove me mad with need. I let loose, grabbing a fistful of her hair as my hips bucked involuntarily. Poppy moaned as my grip tightened, fighting against my hold to take me deeper. Seeing her so desperate for my cock was too much. I lost control, fucking her throat with wild abandonment.

It didn't take long for my balls to tighten, the familiar feeling of my climax drawing near. I didn't even fight it, letting the ecstasy of her mouth consume me. At the last second, I yanked her head back, pulling her off my cock. My other hand reached for my dick, aiming it so my cum sprayed over her bare throat. There wasn't as much as I would have liked since I emptied myself not long ago, but it was enough to paint her a pretty pearl necklace.

"Marry me," I said, like I always did.

Poppy rolled her eyes. "Take your pictures so I can clean up."

Her dry response made me smirk. She heard the line so often, it barely had an effect on her anymore.

Grabbing my phone from my pocket, I held Poppy in place and snapped a few pictures. As always, she humored me, waiting patiently for me to finish collecting my trophies. I then moved them to my special folder so no one could accidentally stumble upon them. These moments were mine and not for anyone else.

"We should probably head back to the party," I said reluctantly.

The last thing I wanted was to join the others. I enjoyed a good party as much as the next person, but holidays like Thanksgiving were never my thing growing up. My family situation didn't exactly make them enjoyable. Poppy changed that when she took over my life, but even then, my happiness was merely an extension of hers. Personally, I would prefer a low-key day eating turkey sandwiches and playing video games.

"Just let me clean up," she replied.

"Of course, I'll go find your plate," I offered.

Reaching out a hand to help her to her feet, my eyes fell briefly down to the mess I made. The neckline of the dress was low enough that I could see it slowly slide down into her cleavage. A piece of me hoped she did a haphazard job cleaning up so some remnants of my claim remained.

Warmth filled me as she placed her hand in mine. Such a simple action and yet it flooded my brain with immense serotonin. It took everything in me to let her go once she was on her feet, severing the connection that made my heart flutter.

"See you out there in a few minutes. Go be a good host," she said, shooing me out of my own room.

I didn't make the fuss that I wanted to, knowing that I was getting what I wanted in the end. I just needed to be patient.

Chapter 11

The Follow Through

Poppy

When I rejoined the festivities, Nixon was sitting on the couch waiting with a plate of food and a glass of wine all laid out in front of him on the coffee table. The moment he saw me, his face lit up, his arms waving excitedly as he beckoned me over. I couldn't help smiling at the goofball.

To my surprise, there were no passing comments or whispering gossip about my prolonged absence as I made my way over to join him. It was strange considering the small scene we made earlier when Nixon dragged me through the house. I knew a good deal of our guests took notice when it happened, yet everyone was too engrossed in their own private conversations to notice me. Even the small crowd around Nixon barely noticed my approach. *Strange.*

When I reached Nixon, he was quick to pull me on his lap, wrapping his arms around me in a tight hug. He nuzzled into my neck, taking in a deep breath and holding it before releasing it with a contented sigh.

"I was starting to worry," Nixon whispered in my ear. The warmth of his voice filled me with a glow as I settled myself more comfortably in his hold.

"Just needed to touch up my makeup. It was a little smudged," I explained. I had been so sure people would be talking, and I didn't want to add any fuel to the fire. *Like a touch up would make it any less obvious. You were MIA for a while.*

"I wonder why," he replied before nipping at the lobe of my ear. The playful gesture sent a shiver over my skin.

I teasingly elbowed Nixon in the side and rolled my eyes, trying to downplay our exchange in front of our guests. Nixon made it very clear that he wanted to be all in, but I was still nervous about the repercussions of what he was asking. It was one thing when it was just the two of us, but a crowd of witnesses complicated things. There would be questions come January, and people who would make assumptions without getting all the facts.

Our inner circle wouldn't think twice when the fake relationship dissolved in January, but there were people present who didn't know how Nixon and I operated. They were the ones who made me nervous. There were bound to be a few well-meaning people who would think they needed to take sides after.

Or maybe everyone will mind their own business. That would be a dream come true, but I doubted it. It was truly surprising how few people grew out of the high school drama mindset. *You can't control other people,* I reminded myself.

My stomach let out an audible grumble, reminding me how famished I was. Without breaking from his conversation with Jack, Nixon rearranged his hold on me so he had a free arm to lean over and grab my plate. I muttered a quiet thank you, not wanting to disrupt his conversation.

The way Nixon tended to my needs like it was second nature made me feel all warm and fuzzy. It wasn't that out of character for him, but after our conversation, things felt different. Maybe it was just me looking at everything differently, but it all felt more intimate.

As if he noticed the shift in my thoughts, Nixon tightened his hold around my waist. It was a silent claim, telling me and everyone else that I belonged to him.

Rupert joined our little crowd around the couch not long after. He wasn't subtle in his displeasure, tossing looks our way every few minutes. Nixon was happy enough to ignore the hulking ginger scowling in our direction, so I tried my best to follow his lead.

My stomach dropped when Rupert leaned in next to Quinn and whispered something I couldn't make out while looking directly at us.

"That's just how they are," she said, laughing in response.

He didn't seem pleased, but left us alone to mingle among the crowd. I made an effort after that to actively avoid him, not wanting to stir up any potential drama.

Meanwhile, the one person I wanted to see, Harrison, was nowhere to be found. I had no idea if he was still even around, not that I could really look with the hold Nixon kept on me. All

I wanted to do was give him a proper apology and explanation without an audience.

As the hours passed by, it was more of the same. I sat and visited while Nixon tended to my every need. There was a rightness to it, but I didn't spend much time dwelling on the feeling. Overthinking things never helped anything.

By the time six rolled around, some of our guests started trickling out. Others stayed and helped clean. Sophie joined me in the kitchen as I scrubbed down the counters while the boys took out the bags upon bags of trash.

"I thought there would be more dishes," she said as she looked around.

"Are you kidding? I've got this down to a science," I explained. "All the bakeware, dishes, and utensils are disposable, which means I only have the dishes from prep, and I clean those as I go."

Nixon and I learned early on that the last thing we wanted to do after hosting such a large gathering was dishes. I made it my mission over the years to find every solution I could to lessen the work after.

"Clever, but it does make a lot of trash," she replied.

"And who is handling that? Not me," I said with a smile.

Sophie laughed and shook her head. "True. When you put it that way, it's brilliant."

I thought that was the end of our conversation, but even with my back turned, I could feel my friend staring. Turning to face her, I leaned against the kitchen counter and folded my arms.

"Spit it out, Sophie."

"It's nothing, but I couldn't help noticing how cozy you and Nixon suddenly were after being gone for a bit. What happened?" she asked. The way her smile stretched ear to ear as her eyes sparkled with excitement was a prime example of what I wanted to avoid.

"The Holiday Pact," I replied deadpan.

Some of the mirth faded from her expression. "That's all?"

"That's all," I confirmed, even if I wasn't sure myself.

Sophie nodded, noticeably disappointed, but she didn't argue or try to convince me there was something more. Hopefully, everyone else would be as respectful about it.

When the guys returned, Nixon came up behind me and wrapped his arms around me. My skin pebbled as he pushed back my hair, trailing kisses from my neck down to my shoulder. His advances in front of the others had been slowly escalating, like he was testing the waters to see how much I would allow.

I reciprocated, pushing my ass against him. A small moan slipped from my lips as I felt his swelling erection press into me. My body craved to feel him inside me, to feel his length stretching me as he filled my wet pussy.

Nixon took it as permission to push the envelope further, his hands roaming my body over the fabric of my dress as he softly bit my neck. A shiver of need coursed through me as my arousal pooled between my thighs.

I teasingly tried to put some space between us, but Nixon held me close. His fingers dug into my hips as he began to rut against my ass. It didn't matter that we were both fully clothed in the middle of our kitchen. The desire between us was too great.

I was ready to hop on the counter and demand Nixon get to work when Jack cleared his throat, reminding me we were not alone. Coming to my senses, I saw Jack, Sophie, and Rupert all staring in our direction with mixed expressions. I tried to step away and feign embarrassment, but Nixon wouldn't let me go.

"We should probably get going. It looks like you crazy kids need some time alone," Jack said, trying to cut the tension.

My cheeks burned as I slowly came to terms with the fact we were dry humping with an audience. Aside from Nixon's almost painful grip on me, he didn't seem affected at all.

"Yeah. Thanks for coming. We got it from here," Nixon replied, his voice way too calm and cheerful.

Sophie winked at me and waved before turning to leave, while Jack just shook his head. Rupert stood there for a second, an almost disappointed look on his face, before he turned and walked away. The sadness in his eyes felt like a punch in the gut.

"You should walk the guests out," I suggested.

"Jack and Sophie have a key. Let them finish clearing the place out for us," Nixon replied.

He leaned, peppering kisses down my neck as his hands found their way under my dress. It was clear where his mind was, but the moment was broken for me.

"You should at least say bye to Rupert. You are the one who invited him," I pushed.

Nixon dropped his hands, taking a step back as he let out an annoyed sigh. "I know what you are doing, Pops."

"I'm not doing anything," I said, though we both knew that wasn't true.

Despite his efforts, Nixon couldn't hide his hurt and frustration. My Nixy was an open book. His eyes darkened, a sign of the coming storm brewing in his heart.

"If you don't want this, then just tell me instead of dragging it out. You know you can be honest with me," he said, gripping the counter next to me.

The accusation stung. It wasn't that I didn't want this. It was that I still wasn't clear what this was. I felt like the rules were changing, but I was too afraid of what acknowledging those changes would mean to give voice to my concerns.

"I just don't want anyone watching us right now," I said quietly.

It wasn't a complete lie. The fewer witnesses, the less real it felt. The less real it felt, the easier it was to ignore everything else.

Nixon stared at me, frowning as he debated whether or not to accept my flimsy excuse. Finally, the tension in his body eased as he leaned in and gave me a peck on the cheek.

"Fine. Go wait for me in my room while I make sure everyone is gone. You promised me dessert," he said as he walked out of the kitchen.

Alone in the kitchen, I let out a sigh of relief. It wasn't that I didn't want Nixon or the pact. I just had too many thoughts swirling in my head, and Rupert looking like a kicked puppy wasn't helping. What I needed was to turn my brain off, or find something else to focus on.

The new toy, I thought to myself as a smile tugged at my lips. Yes, the new toy!

Chapter 12

Preparation

Poppy

Nixon said to wait in his room, so naturally I went to my room instead. If I did as he asked, it would have set the wrong tone for the rest of the evening. The easiest way to quiet all the thoughts and uncertainties that were invading my mind was to distract myself. The easiest way to distract myself was to make my bestie my bitch in the bedroom.

Retrieving my toy box from under the bed, I rummaged through and pulled out everything I needed. Once the items were laid out neatly on the bedside table, I sat on the edge of the bed and waited.

Excitement built up inside me, already providing the distraction I craved. There were no set plans when I selected the toys for the evening. It was a small sampling of a few items. Some, like the paddle, probably wouldn't even be used.

It was only a few minutes before I heard Nixon calling for me.

"Poppy?" His voice carried from down the hall.

I smirked, picturing him standing in his doorway with a look of confusion, or maybe frustration, as he realized I didn't obey. His heavy footsteps grew louder as he drew closer. My heart raced with the anticipation of his arrival.

"Poppy Madison Harper!" he shouted as the door to my room swung open.

I straightened my posture, swapping out my amused expression for something more serious. *Play the role, Poppy.*

"Yes, Nixon Aiden Collins?" I replied with a raised brow.

Nixon's expression turned from frustrated to something more neutral as he took a step inside. His eyes scanned my room, briefly stopping on the table of toys, before moving his focus to me. I didn't react, waiting for him to make the next move.

"I told you my room," he said calmly.

"And I decided my room was better," I replied.

"Is that so?"

He folded his arms, casually leaning against the door frame in some pointless act of defiance. *Or maybe he wants to get a rise out of you.* That wasn't going to happen. I wasn't in the mood for a prolonged standoff or to spend the night taming a brat.

Standing, I smoothed down the skirt of my dress and took one step forward. Nixon watched with an amused smirk like I didn't know how to bring him to his knees. *We'll see about that.*

Walking over to the table, I grabbed two items. When I turned and held them up, his whole demeanor changed. The lax posture straightened as he stood at full attention, his expression more alert.

"Nixy, there are two ways tonight can go," I said.

Raising my left hand, I presented a small, black paddle. His nostrils flared as he tried to hide his emotions. Nixon didn't hate spankings, but it wasn't his preferred form of punishment. You were more likely to get him to comply by withholding pleasure than giving him pain. The paddle was more for show, a symbol of punishment than the tool that would be used.

Next, I raised my right hand, showing him the smooth, black anal vibrator I recently purchased. Nixon's eyes widened as he bit his lip in a poor attempt to disguise his excitement. The vibrator was one he had mentioned in passing a few times, a not-so-subtle hint. I bought it with the intention of surprising him on Christmas Eve, but this felt like a better occasion.

"I can behave." His eyes were glued to the toy as he spoke, like he was having a conversation with it and not me.

"Can you?" I asked as I placed both objects back on the table.

"You know I can, Pops. Nobody is as obedient as me," he replied with a cocky grin.

I had to fight back my smile, amused at how easy it was to break him. He thought he was bragging, no clue he was playing into my plan. Well, what little of a plan I had. There was never any doubt he would fold, but I was a little surprised it happened so quickly after the show he tried to put on.

He tried to watch me as I retook my seat on the bed, but the toys kept stealing his attention. His body was practically vibrating with excitement as he waited to learn how he would earn his reward. *This will be so much fun!*

"Strip for me," I commanded.

"Yes, ma'am." Nixon smiled big and nodded.

Closing his eyes, he slowly inhaled a long breath and held it. His face went slack as he shook his limbs and exhaled. When he opened his eyes, there was a hunger swirling inside them that wasn't there moments ago. My breath caught in anticipation as I waited to see what he would do.

His body started to sway to a silent song that only he could hear. Holding my gaze, his fingers worked the knot in his bowtie. There was nothing inherently sexy about a man loosening a bowtie, but the way Nixon moved his body while he untied it had my attention.

With the bowtie on the floor, he moved on to his shirt. Still watching me, he took his time with each button. I found myself growing impatient at his leisurely pace. The flashes of bare skin as he unbuttoned his shirt were nothing more than a tease. Somehow, despite me calling the shots, Nixon found a way to regain some of the control.

I was salivating by the time the last button was undone. Nixon wasted no time shrugging off his shirt, giving me the view I so desperately wanted.

"Like what you see?" he asked as he seductively ran a hand down his bare chest.

My eyes followed as his hand traveled down the contours of his chiseled abs where the ink of my favorite tattoo was partially exposed. On the outside, I appeared calm and collected, but on the inside, I was drooling like a horny bitch. All I wanted was to drop to my knees and lick my way down his body.

Nixon didn't let my lack of response deter him. He continued his show, unbuckling his belt and sliding it out of the loops. The belt dropped to the ground with a thud, no longer an obstacle in the way.

Nixon gyrated as he popped the button on his skinny jeans. I watched with rapt attention as the zipper lowered. Hooking his fingers under the waistband, he lowered his pants and boxer briefs together with one semi-swift motion. Stepping out of them was a tad less graceful than the rest of his performance, but the end product more than made up for it.

Nixon stood before me naked and partially erect.

"Already excited?" I teased.

"I have a beautiful woman with a nightstand full of toys. What's not to be excited about?" he said.

Grabbing his cock by the base, he stroked himself below the bar on his shaft. My fingers dug into the mattress as I fought the urge to touch my aching clit in response. Tonight was not a night for mutual masturbation, no matter how much I loved watching Nixon get himself off.

"On the bed," I said, straining to get the words out.

Nixon scurried over to the bed and jumped on like an excited puppy. Before I could give him further direction, he was on all fours with his head down and ass in the air.

Grabbing the lube, I spread his cheeks and squeezed out a liberal amount. He sucked in a sharp breath, his asshole puckering as the cool liquid hit his skin.

"Fuck. You need a bottle warmer or something for the lube, Pops," he complained.

I slapped his ass, enjoying the sound of my palm on his meaty flesh.

"Quit your bitching."

"Yes ma'am," he quickly replied.

I reached around with one hand, grabbing his cock by the base and stroking it the way he loved. He moaned in pleasure, rocking his hips to match my rhythm. While he was distracted, I traced the puckered flesh of his ass with my finger, spreading the lube.

Once he relaxed, I slowly pressed in, penetrating the tight ring of muscle. Nixon whimpered, bucking his hips as he sought more.

"So needy," I teased in a soft voice.

The power I felt having full control of my friend's pleasure was indescribable. He was at my mercy, only able to feel as much as I allowed him. To demonstrate my point, I tightened the hand around his cock while my other hand worked his ass.

I took my time, drawing out the motion, as I pushed a single finger inside him, then slowly pulled it back out. Nixon huffed and whimpered in frustration as I repeated the motion over and over at the same slow and steady pace. I was drunk on the power, testing to see how much he would take before he snapped.

"Please, Poppy. You know I need more," he finally begged.

Nixon fisted my sheets, muffled curses falling from his lips as I picked up the pace. I continued to open him up, adding a second finger. By the time I added a third, Nixon was mewling like a cat in heat.

"Don't stop!" he called out as I removed my fingers and released his cock. Nixon was a mess, his muscles locked in position as he panted for breath. "I was so close! Why did you stop?"

I grabbed the vibrator from the table and slid it between his cheeks, lining it up with his entrance but not pressing in.

"I'm sorry. Did you not want to try the new toy?" I asked in a teasing tone.

"No, I do! I'm sorry. I'm so sorry. Please!" He backpedaled quickly.

I smiled as I slid the toy inside him, enjoying the way Nixon squirmed in both pleasure and relief. Once the toy was firmly in place, I hopped off the bed to wash my hands.

"Stay," I commanded before adding, "I'll be right back."

Chapter 13

Satisfaction

Nixon

I lay on the bed, listening to the beating of my heart as I awaited Poppy's return. I should have been frustrated, angry that she stopped when I was mere seconds from coming. Instead, I felt at peace. Soon she would return, and we would continue our game.

The toy was snug inside me, the base curved so it sat flush against my taint. I clenched my ass around the vibrator, enjoying the pleasure that coursed through me each time I did. While I enjoyed getting fucked as much as I enjoyed doing the fucking, there was something special about Poppy being the one penetrating me. With anyone else, anal was a one-way street. Poppy would occasionally receive, but she was never the one to give. I was the only one. That had to mean something.

Her bathroom door creaked as it opened, stealing me from my thoughts. My cock wept for joy as Poppy emerged without a single stitch of clothing. *This was so worth not coming yet.*

I sat up, licking my lips as my eyes roamed over her body. Her ample tits bounced slightly with every step, her nipples hardened into little points. My mouth watered at the thought of sucking on each one until she was squirming and wet.

"You're drooling," she teased as she walked over.

"Because you look delicious," I replied.

She paused by the table next to her bed and picked up a small black object. She pressed a button, and the silicone object nestled inside started to hum. My eyes rolled back, and I let out a groan as the toy vibrated against my prostate. It wasn't very powerful, but it was enough to make my body crave more.

"That's the lowest setting," she explained as she crawled onto the bed. "You'll have to earn the higher settings."

"I'll do anything," I groaned.

Poppy crawled closer. Grabbing my hair with her free hand, she held me in place as she kissed me. I eagerly let her in, moaning into her mouth as she turned up the vibrations. The dual sensations consumed me as I let myself drown in pleasure.

She broke the kiss, leaving me in a breathless daze until I felt a pinch. It was followed by an intense surge of pleasure as she bit my nipple while increasing the vibrations a little more. She wasn't even touching my cock, and yet I felt like I could come from this alone.

I balled my fist in her blankets, fighting the urge to touch her as she alternated her attention between one nipple and the next. I was supposed to be earning my pleasure, but Poppy seemed more than happy to indulge me purely for my reactions. That was more than fine by me. I could sit still like a good boy and let her play with my body.

The toy was amazing. Poppy was amazing. The way she kept me on the edge was amazing. And then it stopped.

She turned off the toy and scooted to the head of the bed, bringing everything to a complete halt. The loss of everything at once hit me like a brick wall. The sudden withdrawal was almost painful.

"What did I do?" I demanded, a bit angry she would just stop like that.

Poppy flashed me a warning look, making me realize my overreaction. I wasn't in the position to make demands, and she didn't deserve to be spoken to that way.

"Sorry, Pops. I'm sorry," I apologized, and I crawled to her. "I shouldn't have spoken to you like that. I forgot myself for a moment."

"I'll say," she replied flatly.

Fuck. That wasn't a good sign.

Desperate to make amends, I leaned down to her ankle and brushed my lips against her skin.

"Please," I begged as I kissed my way up her leg, "please tell me how I might earn your forgiveness."

Her legs fell open in invitation, exposing her glistening pussy, as she raised the remote and clicked the button once. The dull vibration of the lowest setting returned, once again teasing my body with what could be. I didn't need words, her actions were more than clear.

I settled myself between her legs, grabbing her thighs as I dove in. Poppy whimpered as I ran the tip of my tongue teasingly over the slit of her lips. The sound was that of an angel experiencing pure rapture. The vibrations of the toy became more intense as I then ran the flat of my tongue between her folds, lapping at her sex with a mindless hunger.

Pleasing her was already enjoyable, but the addition of my own carnal rewards made it hard to hold back. I became frantic in my efforts, devouring Poppy's perfect pussy like it was my last meal. My fingers dug into the flesh of her thighs, holding her bucking hips in place as I forced my attention on her clit. Her voice was high pitched and almost hoarse as she alternated between cursing me and begging me never to stop.

I was a mindless animal, humping her bed while I continued to assault her with pleasure. Her fingers tangled in my hair as she held me in place, screaming my name. She was close, very close. I needed her over the edge.

I reached down, pressing the sensitive flesh between the cheeks of her ass, but not breaching the tight ring of muscle. Just the tiny bit of pressing was enough to set Poppy off like a firework. Her muscles locked as she shrieked out in pleasure.

That was it. My own orgasm barreled through me, the barrage of sensations sending me into overload. There was nothing I could do to stop it. I emptied my load onto her sheets while my face was buried between her thighs.

When the dust settled, we were both limp and sated. Unable to move, I laid my head on her hip as my dick twitched in response to the toy still vibrating against my prostate.

"Fuck," she said between heavy breaths.

"Fuck, indeed," I agreed.

About the author

Lizzie spends her winter days sipping red wine by the fire while crafting the perfect fictional men for her readers. Her summers are spent exploring the PNW with her family and taking her dogs to the nearby dog park. She has an extensive collection of tokidoki figures that are in no way alarming. It took around two decades to acquire what she has, and is a point of pride. The figures are a much safer topic of discussion than the growing number of pillow boyfriends she has procured.

Learn more about Lizzie and her works at https://lizziebbrown.com.

Also by

Lizzie B Brown